S0-BUA-904

Lots of love, laughter & licks from all your furry friends!

♡ Diane Jaffee ⋄ᵒᵒᵒ

What Did Oliver Do?? is loosely based on true stories of a 95-pound Goldendoodle and his human antics around Breckenridge, Colorado. This book is intended to make everyone laugh out loud at least once just as I do every time I see Oliver in action.

These short tales and illustrations depict many actual events (possibly exaggerated) I observed in Oliver's everyday Breckenridge life. I am so thankful to Steve and Cheryl, his owners, for sharing both Oliver and so many fun times together with our awesome Breckenridge friends.

This was a labor of love and I am grateful to my family (especially Steve for editing and Mom for supporting) and friends who encouraged me to get this written, illustrated, edited and printed in under a year.

A portion of the profits from the sale of this book will be donated to a Breckenridge, Colorado animal rescue group.

Dedication

For Sloan,

A wish for a life filled with love from family and friends,
and a furry dog like Oliver to make you laugh.

To any future grandchildren, I cannot promise a book dedication
(first come first served) but can promise unconditional
love and lots and lots of laughter.

Love, De De

Copyright@2018 Diane S Jaffee
ISBN 978-0-692-19766-0
Printed in the United States
All rights reserved

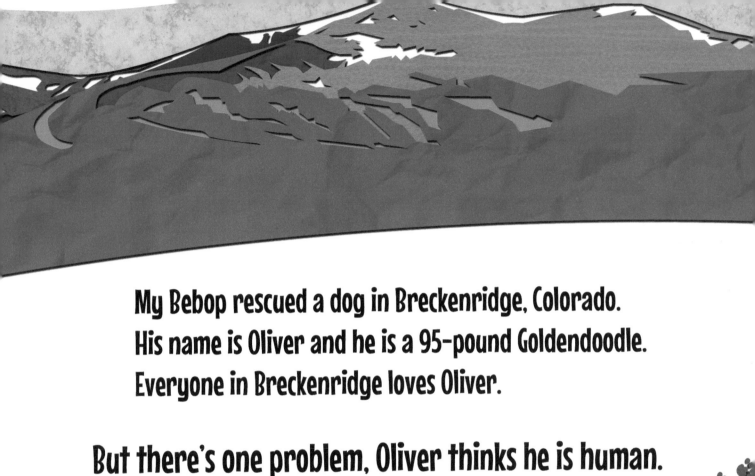

My Bebop rescued a dog in Breckenridge, Colorado.
His name is Oliver and he is a 95-pound Goldendoodle.
Everyone in Breckenridge loves Oliver.

But there's one problem, Oliver thinks he is human.

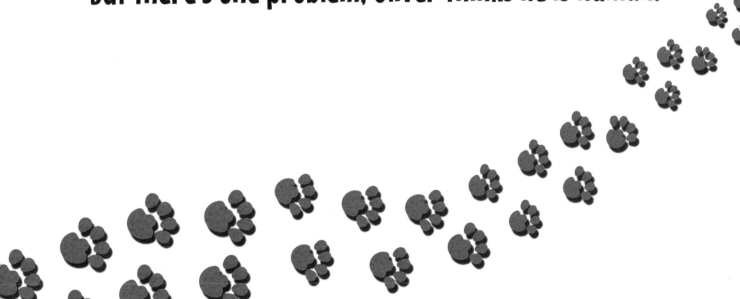

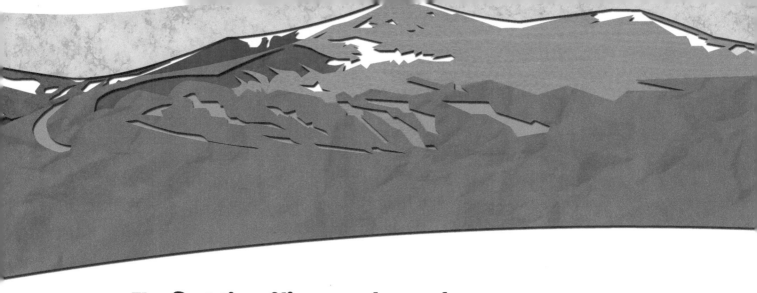

The first time Oliver was home alone,
Bebop left him inside the closed garage.
He had food, water, and a comfy bed.
When we came home, Oliver was gone.

what did Oliver do??

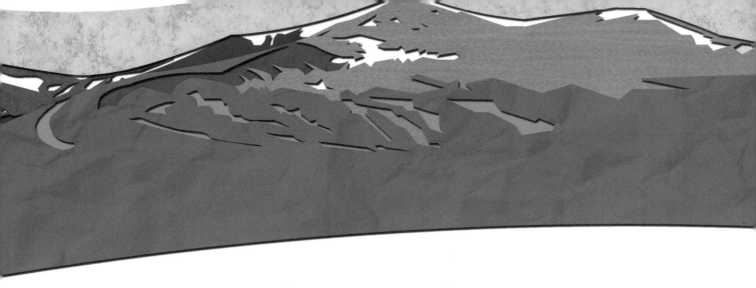

Once we took Oliver on a road trip and stayed in a hotel. We left Oliver in the room and went to eat. When we got back, we were locked out of our room.

what did Oliver do??

Oliver, Bebop and I strolled into town.
When we passed our favorite bakery,
Oliver pulled me right into the store
and straight to the glass display case.

what did Oliver do??

One beautiful summer day we took Oliver hiking.
We spotted workers using an excavator to dig up
dead tree roots. As we got close, they stopped for
a break. Oliver bolted to the excavator.

what did Oliver do??

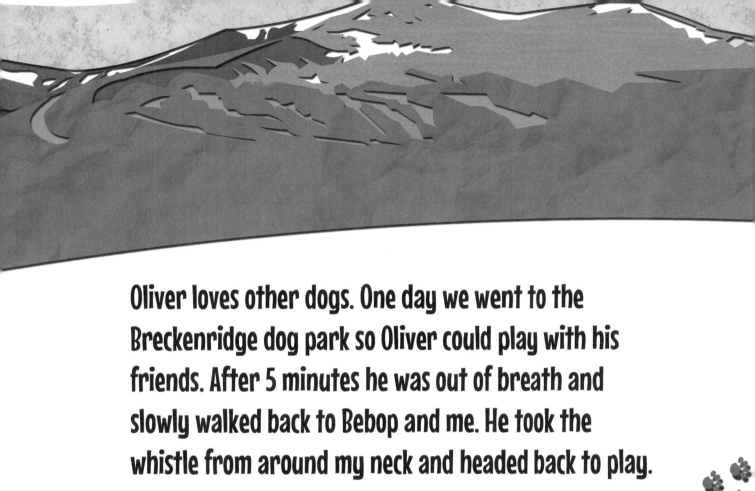

Oliver loves other dogs. One day we went to the Breckenridge dog park so Oliver could play with his friends. After 5 minutes he was out of breath and slowly walked back to Bebop and me. He took the whistle from around my neck and headed back to play.

what did Oliver do??

Oliver likes running errands in the car.
One day Bebop stopped to pick up nails from
the hardware store. When Bebop returned,
his car was not where he had left it.

what did Oliver do??

Oliver loves to swim on a hot summer day. He shows off his dog paddle before getting out to sun himself. I often swim laps beside him. One day, I saw Oliver doing something he had never done before.

what did Oliver do??

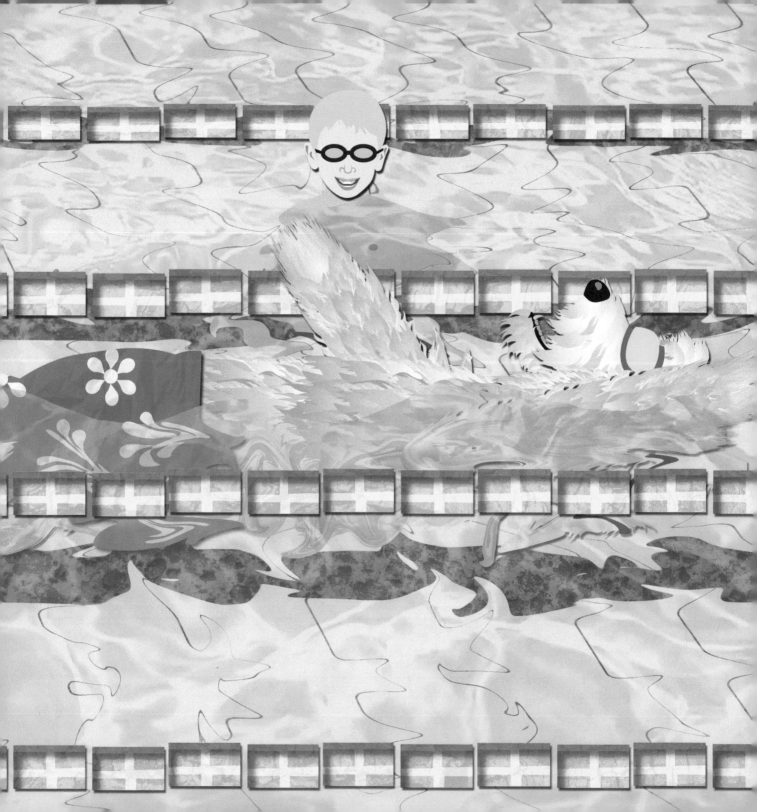

Since Oliver is such a smart dog, Bebop took him to service dog training so he could volunteer with him at our hospital. The patients thought he was the smartest dog they had ever met.

what did Oliver do??

Oliver loves the snow at Bebop's Breckenridge mountain house. One day he watched through the window as we all skied home. We left our skies outside and Oliver came out to play. When I called him he was nowhere to be found.

what did Oliver do??

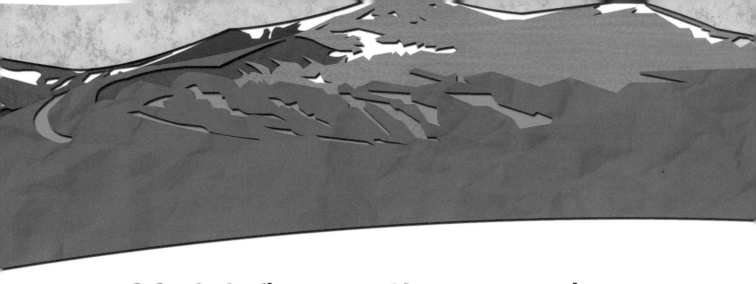

BeBop had a dinner party. We put some appetizers on the dining room table. When I looked over, the smoked salmon was gone.

what did Oliver do??

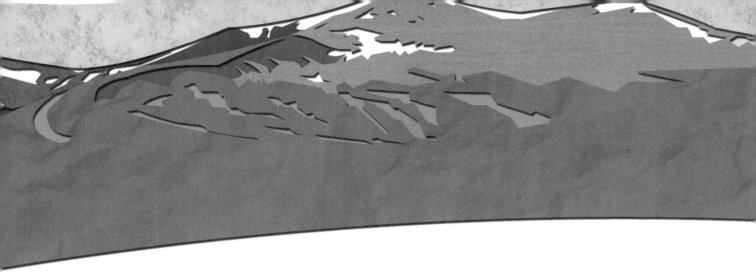

Oliver loves having his teeth brushed.
One day, he came with me to my dentist
appointment. When they called my name,
Oliver ran in to see the dentist.

what did Oliver do??

It's true, Oliver does think he is human.
And, after a long day of mischief and play,
Oliver the Dog
is ready for a good night's rest. I climbed
into bed and said good night to Oliver.

what did Oliver do??

CPSIA information can be obtained
at www.ICGtesting.com
Printed in the USA
BVHW021219010820
585174BV00001B/1